*Dedicated to my loves*
*M.W., B.W., and M.W.Jr.*
*Thank you for all*
*your support.*

# THE SQUIRREL WHO HOMESCHOOLED

*Aunt Olga*
*Thank you for*
*Supporting my dreams*
*Love you forever.*

## by Kacie Washington

### Illustrated by Kath Grimshaw

The air was crisp, and apples were hanging from the trees. There was a boy who was ready to go to school. He packed his backpack, put on his shoes, picked up his lunch, grabbed his coat, and headed to the door.

His mother rushed to stop him. She said, "Did you forget? You're already at school! This year you are going to homeschool." She said, "I am excited to be your teacher! We are going to have fun together."

The boy said, "Mom, you are a ton of fun, but what about my friends?"

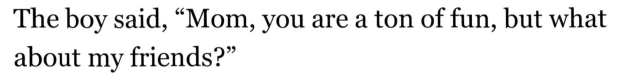

She replied, "You have a sister, she's your forever friend. And a fish, and two cousins, and 1, 2, 3, 4, 5, 6, 7 friends we see for playdates and field trips. Over time you  will meet more friends too."

The boy said, "I guess you're right."

"Well, let's get started. First up, Morning Meeting," said the mom. They sat at the dining room table and started the day. The boy sat by the window that looked into the backyard.

Every day at the same time, the boy noticed
that a squirrel would peek in the window.
Some days he would have a nut, other days
he would just look around.

The boy decided to give him a name: Max McNutty!
Every day the boy would talk to the squirrel, telling him
how he was feeling and what he was doing that day.

Max was a great listener.

One day the boy decided to share what he was learning with the squirrel. The boy told him about how there are 365 days in a year, 7 days in a week, and 24 hours in a day, broken up by day and night.

Max was excited to learn. He took the knowledge and ran as fast as he could across the backyard, up the gate, over the bush, up his tree and into his den. He thought these facts would be important to store for future use.

The next day, the squirrel came back at the same time eager to learn more. This time the boy told Max all about how sharks and alligators like to eat the larger number. And if you add 2 to an even number the answer is always even, and if you add 2 to an odd number the answer is guaranteed to be odd.

The squirrel thought to himself, *I'm not sure how to use these facts just yet, but it's fascinating!* So he rushed off across the backyard, up the gate, over the bush, and up his tree.

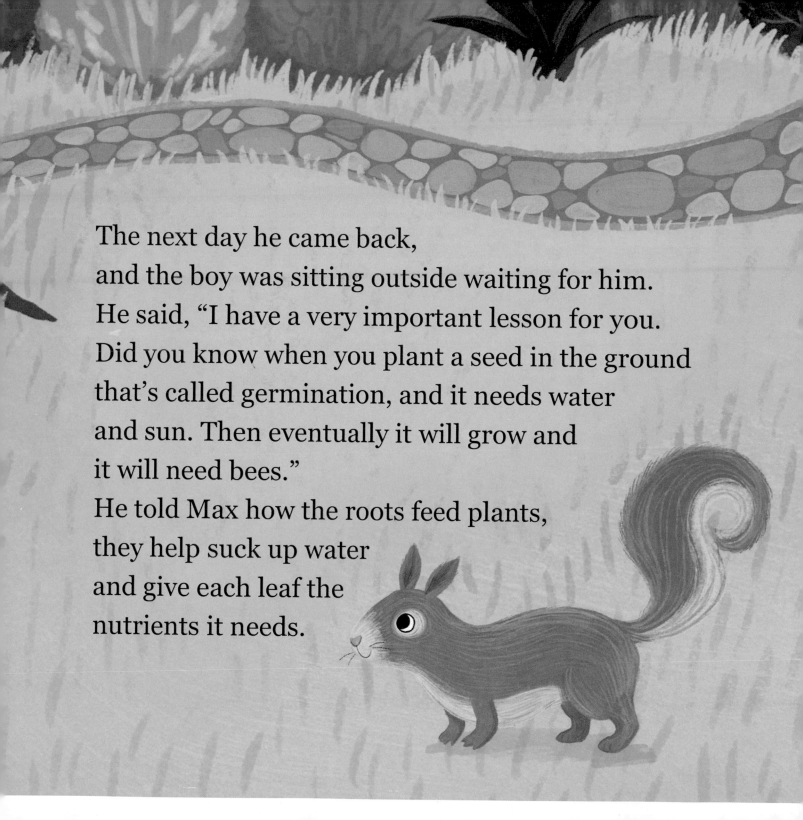

The next day he came back,
and the boy was sitting outside waiting for him.
He said, "I have a very important lesson for you.
Did you know when you plant a seed in the ground
that's called germination, and it needs water
and sun. Then eventually it will grow and
it will need bees."
He told Max how the roots feed plants,
they help suck up water
and give each leaf the
nutrients it needs.

The squirrel thought, *This is great news. Now I know how to make my food grow!* He was so excited he could hardly stand it. He ran as fast as he could across the backyard, up the gate, over the bush and up his tree, where he treasured the lesson he learned. The squirrel was so grateful.

The next day Max went back to the window. He smelled the most delightful aroma coming from inside. The boy came to the window and said, "I have something very important to tell you. If you ever get bored eating apples, you can make apple chips. All you do is slice them thin, add a pinch of sugar, a pinch of cinnamon, a pinch of salt, mix them up, then lay them on a pan covered with parchment paper. Bake them at 250 degrees for 90 minutes. Then, voilà! You have delicious apple chips and a home that smells delightful."

The squirrel was overjoyed. Sometimes he did get bored with plain apples. He set out across the backyard, up the gate, over the bush, and up his tree where he treasured all his information from his friend.

He thought how grateful he was for all the lessons the boy was sharing. He decided he would bring a gift and say thank you. The next day Max took a peanut to the window. The boy was excited and said to the squirrel, "Gracias por el maní, which is Spanish for 'thank you for the peanut.'" The squirrel was tickled by the boy's response. He took his new words and ran as fast as he could across the backyard, up the gate, over the bush, and up his tree.

The boy knew all the facts he was sharing with the squirrel were gifts his mother shared with him. The boy wondered, *how can I be as thoughtful as Max? How can I show my gratitude to my mom?* He thought long and hard about something she might love.

*He could draw a picture?* Then he decided that would not do.

*Maybe a song? No,* he thought. *That won't do either.*

*Hmmm, what about cereal in bed? Nope, not that either.*

He suddenly said, "I've got it, the thing she loves most!" So the boy ran across the house, up the stairs, over the sofa, and into the living room where his mother was watering her plants.

He reached up and gave her a big, tight hug and said, "Thank you for all the things you teach me."

His mother smiled and said, "I love you.
You're welcome, and the pleasure is mine."

The next day when the boy
sat at the table for school, he
looked up and noticed the
backyard was filled with
squirrels waiting for the
boy to teach them
something new.

Kacie Washington is a wife and mother of two fun-finders. She is passionate about children developing as confident readers and has launched, volunteered, worked, and served on the board for several organizations to help make that a reality in her hometown, Seattle WA.

As a teen Kacie volunteered as a Team Read reading coach to elementary school students before earning her BA in Communications from Seattle Pacific University. After graduating she returned to Team Read to serve on their Board and help guide the organization to continued success. Kacie also spent several years at the YMCA developing youth learning programs before changing course to become a homeschooling mom of two. The joy she gets from seeing her own children's excitement with reaching new heights in reading proficiency inspired her to begin writing and sharing her own books. Her hope is that children and parents will find similar adventure and joy in reading.

When she's not writing, you can find her cooking with her children or hosting a party for friends and family. Kacie is a champion of turning dreams into reality.

*kaciewashington.com*